One Hundred Shining Candles

One Hundred Shining Candles

by JANET LUNN   illustrated by LINDSAY GRATER

TUNDRA BOOKS

Published in Canada by Tundra Books,
75 Sherbourne Street, Toronto, Ontario M5A 2P9

Published in the United States by Tundra Books of Northern New York,
P.O. Box 1030, Plattsburgh, New York 12901

Library of Congress Control Number: 2007908619

Library and Archives Canada Cataloguing in Publication
Lunn, Janet, 1928-
    One hundred shining candles / Janet Lunn ; illustrated by Lindsay Grater.

Originally published: Toronto : Lester & Orpen Dennys, 1990.
ISBN 978-0-88776-889-7
    1. Christmas stories, Canadian (English) I. Grater, Lindsay, 1952-
II. Title.
PS8573.U55O53 2008   jC813'.54   C2007-906796-4

We acknowledge the financial support of the Government of Canada through the Book Publishing Industry Development Program (BPIDP) and that of the Government of Ontario through the Ontario Media Development Corporation's Ontario Book Initiative. We further acknowledge the support of the Canada Council for the Arts and the Ontario Arts Council for our publishing program.

ONTARIO ARTS COUNCIL
CONSEIL DES ARTS DE L'ONTARIO

The illustrations for this book were rendered in watercolor and graphite

Printed and bound in Singapore

1 2 3 4 5 6   13 12 11 10 09 08

For all my grandchildren
– JL

For Christopher
– LG

hristmas was coming. Snow lay thick on the branches in the deep woods and whitened the log cabins in the clearings.

In the schoolmaster's house, the children were listening, spellbound. The schoolmaster was talking about Christmas. Lucy had stopped listening. For the first time in her ten-year-old life, Lucy, with her tight black braids and her neatly tucked-in collar, was lost in a dream.

"Candles," Mr. Jones had said. "I have seen one hundred candles lighted to celebrate the birth of our Lord. In big cities, I have seen red silk ribbons and dark green cedar festooning the rooms of grand houses. I have seen roast goose and steaming plum puddings set out on long tables. I have seen gifts, wagons, spinning tops, and dolls . . ."

"Please, sir?" It was Dan. "What did all the candles look like all lighted?" Lucy was surprised. It wasn't like her little brother to speak out in school. Dan's blue eyes were shining.

"Oh," – the old man's voice was soft – "the whole room was aglow. There was golden light even in the darkest corners. It was elegant! Most elegant!"

Lucy said nothing to Dan all the way home, along the path through the dark forest.

She knew there wouldn't be steaming pudding and roast goose in their cabin in the backwoods of Upper Canada. Maybe some folks in the village might have them, but not the Jamieson family. There was no money to spare, with Ma sick and Pa so worried.

"I'm sorry," Pa had told the children. "There will be no presents this Christmas. All we can manage is the bread." For as long as Lucy could remember, Ma had baked white bread for Christmas – two loaves – a big one for the family and a small one for the birds. White flour was costly, but when Pa had suggested not having it this year, Ma had said she'd sooner not eat for a week than do without their Christmas bread. Dan had said he'd give his penny for the white flour.

"No, Dan." Pa had been firm. "Grandpa gave you that penny because you were named for him. You keep it."

Lucy longed for something like Dan's penny to offer – even if Pa turned it back.

All evening, Lucy was thinking. She was thinking while she cooked the cornmeal stir-about in the big iron pot that hung over the fire. She was thinking while she put away the flax her mother had been spinning and while she tidied up for the night.

When, at last, she had finished her chores, she hung her one carefully mended dress on its peg over her bed. And with a smile on her face, she lay down to sleep. She had a plan, a wonderful, exciting plan.

Pa left early the next morning to take the wheat to the mill to be ground. He would be away for almost two days. The children went outside to see him off. "If you hear bears or wolves up close, bar the door," he told them. "And you're to mind your ma, and do as you know you ought." Pa turned and was off through the woods.

Lucy waited until she could no longer hear the crunch of snow under his boots. She grabbed Dan's hand and pulled him over behind the woodpile. "I've got a plan," she whispered, barely able to control her excitement. She told him about her wonderful idea.

"Candles!" breathed Dan. "It will be light everywhere. It will be light even behind the maple-sugar bin, Lucy!"

"And you're not to let on, Dan," Lucy ordered. "It's to be a surprise. I wouldn't have told you, except I knew you'd see me making them. You're not to leak out a single word, and you're not to give out any of those I-know-a-secret looks, either." Lucy's dark eyes were fierce.

"I won't. I promise. But we'll have to have tallow and wicks to make the candles. Will Pa be angry we took them without asking?"

"Pa's gone, and when he comes back it will be done, and he won't know till Christmas. Then he'll be more'n pleased to see Ma so happy." Lucy's voice was so firm, Dan dared say no more about Pa.

"Can I help?" he asked.

Lucy didn't want him to help. The candles were her idea, her present. But Dan's blue eyes were so big and so full of longing. She sighed. "Oh, all right. But mind, you've got to be very careful. If you mess it up, I'll skin you and boil you up for Christmas dinner!"

That evening after school, the children sat on the woodpile, wriggling their toes in their thin boots, plotting their candle making until their teeth chattered with the cold and the moon had risen over the big tamarack tree behind the shed. Lucy said Dan could gather the candle frame, the wick, and the tallow from the shed and hide them in the small soap kettle that was kept there.

As for the candles – "They got to be red," they agreed. "Red like the columbine and the sumac," said Dan.

"We'll make them red with Ma's red madder dye," said Lucy. She looked at her old faded dress. The dye was to have been used for a new red dress in the spring.

"I'll fetch it down," Dan offered bravely. The dye crock was in a niche over the fireplace in the cabin.

"No. It was my idea, so I'll do the hard part," Lucy declared.

That night Lucy lay in her bed watching the dancing flames in the fireplace make shadows on the dark wall of the cabin. At first, the shadows looked like herself, reaching stealthily toward the niche in the stone chimney. Then they changed into Ma and Pa, looking at her with reproach. She yanked the bedcovers up over her head.

Lucy woke at first light and remembered at once what she had to do. She looked across the room. Ma was still asleep. Swiftly and silently, she crept from her bed. She was up on the chair and down again with the dye crock in her hands. In a flash she had the chair in its place, the crock under her bed, and was back under the covers. She remembered the tinderbox to light the fire with. Up she jumped! She flew to the chair, up to the niche, got down with the tinderbox, and back in bed just as her mother yawned her first yawn.

That afternoon the children raced home from school. They whistled through their chores with such speed that their mother said, "I believe you could raise a barn, just the two of you, if you had a mind to."

Lucy decided they must build the fire behind the house so Ma would not see the smoke. She bustled about, telling Dan what to do and how to do it. Dan lugged the logs from the woodpile and the kettle full of candle-making things from the shed. He set the kettle over the logs and, with great ceremony, Lucy lit the fire. In a few moments it was blazing around the kettle.

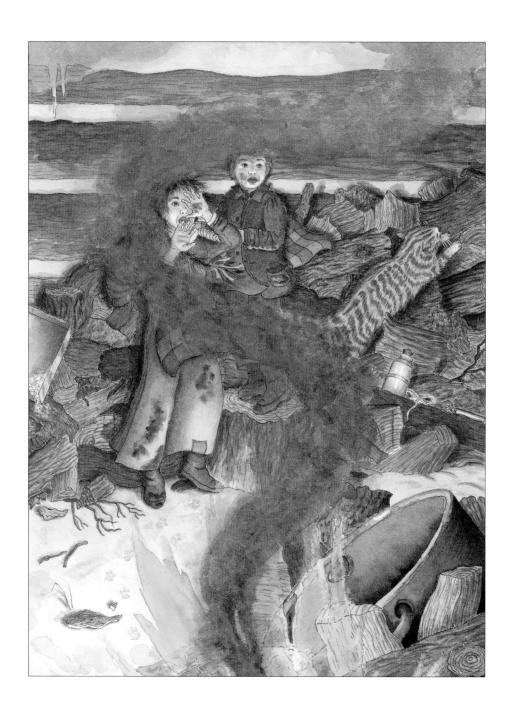

"Now stand back, Dan. Not there – out of the way, over there. Don't you go messing it all up." But it wasn't Dan, serious and intent, who sent their dream up in smoke. It was Lucy, with her busying and bossing. When she figured the kettle was good and hot, she threw in the lump of tallow and stirred it so hard she knocked the kettle askew. She tried to straighten it. The kettle tilted. The tallow fell into the fire. At once, a billow of stinking black smoke rose from the flames.

The children stood rooted to the ground. Tears from the smoke ran down their smudged faces.

"I've ruined it," whispered Lucy. "I've ruined Christmas." She couldn't even cry, the feeling was so deep and dismal. Together, the children sat down on a rock, feeling colder and more miserable than two people had ever felt before, or since.

"It ain't ruined, Lucy," Dan said. "I got an idea. I can get some more tallow from Mr. Bosey."

"Mr. Bosey?"

"Pa said once that Mr. Bosey would give up his coat for a penny in his pants' pocket, and I've got my penny. I reckon Mr. Bosey will be glad to give me some tallow for it."

"No! You can't give up your penny!"

"Yes, I can!" Dan's voice was trembling. "Pa said Grandpa said I was to have something special with my penny, and I want us to have red candles for Christmas."

Dan ran toward the bay. Mr. Bosey lived on the other side, but because the bay was frozen, it wouldn't take more than fifteen minutes to get across and back.

Lucy knew Mr. Bosey would give Dan the tallow. But Dan's penny would be gone, and it was her fault. "I figured I was so almighty fine. But it was me that ruined it!"

She was still wrapped up in her own bleak feelings when Dan came running back. He thrust a pan of tallow into her hands.

"He wants the pan back, the old skinflint!" Dan was breathless. And he was shining so with his desire to make the candles that Lucy threw her arms around him and hugged him tight. Dan was so surprised that his face turned redder than the madder dye.

This time they worked together – and with great care. Lucy made sure the kettle was steady over the fire, and Dan put the tallow into it.

Like two witches they crouched over their cauldron, watching the white tallow melt and bubble. Then they took the candle frame, which Lucy had threaded with five lengths of wick, and Lucy dipped them slowly into the hot tallow. She lifted them out into the cold air so the tallow would harden. She dipped again and again until the candles were almost thick enough. It was time to add the color.

"You do it," said Lucy. "You do it, because you gave up your penny."

So Dan stirred in the dye and
dipped the candles once more.
He pulled them out.

"Lucy," he wailed. "It won't mix!
The candles are all splotchy!"

"Hush! You want Ma to hear?"
Lucy whispered hoarsely. "Just you
go ahead and dunk them candles.
Just you dunk and dunk."

Dan dunked and dunked. When he was finished he held up the candles. They were mottled red and white, and they weren't nearly as straight as the candles Pa made. And there weren't a hundred – only five. Mr. Bosey had given Dan just that much tallow for his penny.

But Dan and Lucy didn't mind anymore. They scraped the last of the red-and-white tallow onto their candles with a stick and held them up in the frosty evening air to harden. Then they sat back on their heels and admired their handiwork.

They put out the fire with handfuls of snow. With great care, they placed their candles in the tin box Lucy kept her treasures in – to keep them safe from nibbling mice – and stowed the tin in a chink in the wall of the shed.

The next day, Pa came home with two sacks over his shoulders – the big one full of the coarse brown flour the family always used, the small one full of fine white flour for the Christmas bread.

"Here's Christmas," he said, handing the small sack to Ma. Dan looked at Lucy and quickly looked away again. But he didn't give away their secret.

The day before Christmas, Ma mixed the special dough, kneading it over and over until it was soft and smooth. She baked it into two delicious-smelling loaves – the small one for the birds, the big one for the family. Together, Lucy and Dan went out and cut a few pine and cedar boughs to place on the mantel and over the door and window frames.

Finally, it was Christmas morning. Fresh snow had fallen in the night, covering the world with glistening magic.

The children tiptoed from their beds before dawn, even before Pa was up. Outside, all was silent with the silence that comes with deep, soft snow. In that silence, they set their candles in a row on the table and lit them.

"Ma," Dan called quietly, but their mother was already standing beside him. Pa was right behind her. No one said anything. Lucy turned, suddenly scared, to see what her mother and father were thinking. She saw, in her mother's eyes, the same glowing look she had seen in Dan's eyes when Mr. Jones had told them about the candles. And Pa? Well, Pa's eyes looked softer than Lucy had seen them since Ma had got sick.

Lucy could contain herself no longer. She took Dan's hands and began to dance around and around the table, telling all about Mr. Jones's stories and the spilled tallow and Dan's penny and Mr. Bosey and the madder-root dye until everyone was laughing. Pa laughed loudest of all. He lifted Dan onto his shoulders, marched him around the room, and said he thought this was surely the best use in all the world a body could put to a penny.

Ma smiled and smiled, and the whole room was bright with the light of one hundred shining candles.